PUPPY POWER!

BOOKS IN THE PUPPY PATROL SERIES ™

COMING SOON

PUPPY PATROL ™
PUPPY POWER!

JENNY DALE

Illustrations by Mick Reid
Cover illustration by Michael Rowe

AN
APPLE
PAPERBACK

SCHOLASTIC INC.
New York Toronto London Auckland Sydney
Mexico City New Delhi Hong Kong Buenos Aires

No part of this publication may be reproduced, in whole or in part, or stored in a
retrieval system, or transmitted in any form or by any means, electronic,
mechanical, photocopying, recording, or otherwise, without written permission
of the publisher. For information regarding permission,
write to Macmillan Publishers Ltd., 20 New Wharf Rd.,
London N1 9RR Basingstoke and Oxford.

ISBN 0-439-45351-8

All rights reserved. Published by Scholastic Inc., 557 Broadway,
New York, NY 10012 by arrangement with Macmillan Children's Books,
a division of Macmillan Publishers Ltd.

12 11 10 9 8 7 6 5 4 3 2 1   3 4 5 6 7 8/0

Printed in the U.S.A.   40
First Scholastic printing, July 2003

SPECIAL THANKS TO CHERITH BALDRY

CHAPTER ONE

"**D**one!" said Neil Parker. He leaned on the mop and pushed a hand through his spiky brown hair. "OK, Mom?"

Carole Parker turned away from the oven to look at the wet kitchen floor. "That'll do. Thanks, Neil. And next time, keep an eye on Jake, will you?"

Neil put the mop away and tipped the bucket of dirty water into the sink. "Well, *you* left the strawberry shortcake where Jake could get it," he said in an injured voice.

Carole smiled. "That's true. I should have been more careful!"

Neil's younger sister, ten-year-old Emily, looked up from the animal magazine she was reading at the table. "I blame this awful rain. If we could have taken Jake out, it wouldn't have happened."

"He was bored," Neil agreed.

Jake, Neil's young black-and-white Border collie, had managed to eat nearly half the strawberry shortcake Carole had made for dessert before anybody noticed and stopped him. He had obviously felt very ill afterward and ended up getting sick all over the kitchen floor. Bob Parker, Neil's dad, had taken him straight to Mike Turner, the local vet, while Neil cleaned up the mess. Five-year-old Sarah, the youngest member of the Parker family, had gone along, too.

"Well, what's done is done," Carole said. "Don't worry, Neil. Mike will make sure that Jake's alright."

Bob and Carole Parker ran King Street Kennels and Rescue Center, just outside the small country town of Compton. Dogs were very important to Neil, and Jake was the most special dog of them all. Neil wouldn't feel happy until he had Jake back — along with Mike Turner's guarantee that the mischievous young dog had recovered from his experience.

Restlessly, Neil wandered over to the kitchen window and stared out. Rain was pouring down from a dull gray sky, dripping off the eaves of the kennel buildings and splashing into the puddles that covered the courtyard outside. Even the essential kennel work was difficult on such a wet day, and it was impossible to take the dogs for long walks. Neil wondered how much longer everybody would be stuck indoors before it stopped.

"Cheer up," Emily said. "Think about something else. Think about our party."

Neil brightened up. "I just heard from Max," he said. "He finished filming the other day, so he's going to come here on Tuesday and stay over for the party next weekend."

Max Hooper and his golden cocker spaniel, Prince, were the stars of Neil and Emily's favorite TV program, *The Time Travelers*. Max had become friendly with the Parkers when he had filmed an episode at Padsham Castle, near Compton, and now Neil felt that celebrations at King Street were not complete unless Max was there to share them.

"That's great," said Carole. "Now, take a look at these. The White Rose Hotel has just sent me some suggestions for menus, so we can decide what we'd like to eat that day."

She put several sheets of paper on the kitchen table and spread them out for Neil and Emily to see.

Emily pored over them eagerly. "Cucumber mousse? That sounds really gross!"

"Are we really going to the White Rose Hotel?" Neil said doubtfully. "Mom, it's so expensive."

"Well, it's a special party," Carole said. "Your dad and I have been married for fifteen years, and we've been running King Street for ten. That's worth celebrating somewhere special, isn't it? I want all our friends in Compton to celebrate with us."

"Yes, I know, but — well, the White Rose Hotel won't let dogs in, will it? And it won't be a real party without dogs."

"Ah, but that's the genius of it," Carole said, smiling. "The party won't be in the hotel itself. They've got that beautiful garden in the back, with the stream running along the border, and they're going to serve us a buffet dinner — for people *and* dogs. And don't worry — you'll get to invite some of *your* friends, too!"

"Cool!" said Neil, his face splitting into a huge grin. He bent over the hotel menus along with Emily. "I don't see anything here about what the dogs are going to eat."

"How typical of you, Neil," said Carole, "to think about the dogs before —" She broke off at the sound of the front door opening.

"Jake!" cried Neil, springing to his feet.

He headed for the hallway, but before he reached it, his sister Sarah ran into the kitchen and shook herself like a dog, scattering raindrops everywhere.

"Hey!" said Emily, protecting the menus.

Bob Parker followed Sarah into the kitchen.

The young Border collie was nowhere to be seen.

"Where's Jake?" Neil asked, feeling frightened.

"It's OK, Neil," Bob said. "Don't panic. Mike examined Jake and says he should be fine. He's just keeping him overnight just to be sure that everything is out of his system and to check that his digestive system hasn't suffered any damage. It got quite a shock today. Mike will give him some medicine to settle his stomach. Jake'll be able to rest quietly at the clinic and he can't get into any more trouble there."

"OK." Neil let out a sigh of relief. All the same, he wanted to see Jake for himself. It seemed like a long time until the next day and the house already felt empty without his lively doggy friend.

While Carole made Sarah take off her coat and

hang it up, Bob took an old towel and rubbed his curly brown hair and beard.

"It's getting worse out there," he said. "See how wet we got just coming in from the car? There are fallen branches all along Compton Road."

"It's not fair," said Neil. "Why does it have to rain on the weekend? It was nice out all week when we had to go to school."

"I know," said Carole. "And it's supposed to be the beginning of summer. But just look at it! What worries me is whether we'll be able to have our party outdoors."

"It can't go on raining like this for much longer," Bob said reassuringly. "There's plenty of time before we need to worry about the party."

When Neil came downstairs the next morning, he heard the radio playing in the kitchen. His mother had made scrambled eggs, and the rest of the family had already started eating breakfast. Outside, the sky was still grim and the rain was still falling.

"I just heard the weather forecast," Carole said. "They think the weather's going to get *worse.*"

"Fudge hates the rain," Sarah announced.

"Fudge can go to sleep in his nice warm straw," said Bob with a grin. "There are times when I wish *I* were a hamster."

"Dad, we'll still be able to pick up Jake, won't we?"

Neil asked anxiously as he took his seat and reached for the cereal box.

"Yes, we'll be able to pick up Jake," said Bob. "Right after breakfast, before the obedience class."

"Do you think people will come out for the class this morning, in weather like this?" Carole asked.

"Well, I still have to be here, just in case," said Bob, pouring himself a cup of tea. "If anyone can't make it, they'll give us a call."

"I could sit in the office by the phone," Emily offered. "I'll update the web site. There's nothing else to do on a day like this."

When breakfast was over, Neil put on his boots and waterproof jacket and splashed across the driveway to the Range Rover with his father. Bob pulled out in the direction of Compton and drove slowly along the wet road with the windshield wipers hissing back and forth. Water was gurgling along in the gutters on either side, and the road was slippery with mud and leaves.

"This is nasty," Bob muttered, concentrating on his driving. "I figure if we —"

He stopped what he was saying as the car turned a corner. Just ahead was a line of cars inching their way along in the direction of Compton. Bob slowed down as he joined the line.

"What's the matter?" Neil asked, trying to peer past the car in front to see more of the road ahead.

Bob didn't answer. A moment later, as they crept around the next bend at the top of the hill that led down into Compton, Neil could see what was causing the backup.

At the bottom of the hill, a few hundred yards away, water was covering the road in a wide gray pool. A police car was parked beside it, and as they drew closer, Neil could make out a policeman in a bulky yellow waterproof jacket putting up detour signs. The traffic was turning right along a narrow lane.

"The road's flooded!" Neil exclaimed.

Bob pulled over to the side of the road and started to reverse into a driveway.

"Hey, Dad!" Neil said. "What are you doing?"

"Going home, Neil. I'm sorry, but it'll take hours to get into town along the side streets. I have to get back to the kennel for the class."

"But what about Jake?"

"Jake will be fine. I know you want him back, Neil," Bob went on as Neil started to protest, "but it's just not possible right now. You can call Mike when we get home."

Neil had to admit his dad was right, and he didn't argue as the car turned around and they cautiously set off back the way they had come. He was missing Jake, but he knew his dad had to put the kennel first.

Bob parked the car in the garage and tramped through the rain to the barn where the obedience classes were held. Neil made a dash for the door of the office, and let himself in. Emily was sitting at the desk with the computer on.

When Neil appeared she asked anxiously, "Didn't you pick up Jake?"

"No. But there isn't a problem — not with Jake." Neil explained about the flood and the detour. "We had to come back so Dad could run the class," he finished.

"Three people have called to cancel," said Emily, picking up the notepad beside the phone. "I'd better tell Dad."

"No, I'll tell him," Neil said with resignation. "I'm wet already."

He took the piece of paper Emily gave him and braved the weather again, hunching his shoulders as he ran to the barn. A cold wind was sweeping the rain across the courtyard, rippling the sheet of water that covered it. *What if the water gets into the kennel blocks?* he asked himself. *Where will the dogs go then?*

The barn was warm and dry inside. Bob was standing near the door, talking to a woman who had just arrived for the class. As Neil went in, her young corgi jumped up and rushed toward him, pulling at his leash.

Neil squatted down in front of him. "Hi, Tod. Re-member me?" He fished out one of the dog treats he always carried in his pocket and gave it to the corgi, stroking his smooth golden-brown fur.

"I couldn't decide whether to come, Mr. Parker," Tod's owner, Mrs. Chisolm, was saying. "It's no joke driving in this weather. I had to come over the river, and the water level is right up to the banks."

That reminded Neil about the cancellations, and he handed the piece of paper to his father. Bob glanced at it and stuck it in his pocket.

"Looks as if we'll be a small group this morning," he said to Mrs. Chisolm. "But that's OK. At least King Street Kennels is still open for business."

* * *

"Dad, we've got to pick up Jake!" Neil said urgently as he packed his schoolbag the next morning. "Can't we stop at Mike's on the way to school?"

There had been no time to even think about a visit to Mike Turner's clinic for the rest of Sunday. The Parkers were kept busy with the routine kennel work, which was much harder in the pouring rain. All the boarding and rescue dogs were getting restless because they couldn't get their proper exercise.

"OK," said Bob. "But only if it won't make you late. Otherwise I'll pick him up on my way back."

Relieved to be fetching his beloved dog at last, Neil put on his boots and parka and hurried out to the car. The rain was still pelting down. Sarah danced around in the driveway, splashing in the puddles. "I'm singing in the rain! Just singing in the rain!" she sang.

"Give it a rest," Emily muttered as she shoved her little sister into the backseat of the Range Rover and climbed in herself.

Neil got in beside Bob, and the car pulled out cautiously into the road. By now, the gutters were overflowing and water was streaming along the road itself. Bob crawled along at a slow speed, peering through the windshield, until he reached the top of the hill.

Suddenly, he braked. Neil was thrown forward against his seat belt. "Dad!" he protested — and then saw what was in front of him. "Wow!" he exclaimed.

"I can't believe it!" Emily added from behind him.

The pool at the foot of the hill where the police had placed the detour signs had spread along the road and into the fields on either side. The water was murky and it looked very deep. Farther away, where the river normally could be seen winding around Compton, was another expanse of water, stretching right up to the town itself. From what Neil could see, some of the low-lying houses were already flooded. A local church, on a hill in the middle of the town, rose up out of the waters like a huge beached ship.

Compton was surrounded by water.

CHAPTER TWO

As the Parkers' Range Rover turned into the driveway at King Street Kennels, Carole appeared at the front door.

"Thank goodness you're back!" she said as everyone piled out of the car and dashed for shelter through the driving rain. "I heard on the radio that the riverbanks have burst. They say some parts of town will have to be evacuated."

"I'm not surprised," said Bob as he pulled off his soaked coat. "It looks like the North Sea down there!"

"The school secretary just called," said Carole. "School's closed until the floods go down."

At any other time, Neil would have been elated to hear that. Now, he couldn't think of anything but Jake. He wished he had tried harder the day before to get to Mike Turner's to pick him up, but there had been so much to do, and he had never imagined that the water would rise as high as this. Fortunately, King Street Kennels was on the higher ground on the outskirts of Compton and was unlikely to be affected.

"Dad," he asked, "what about Jake?"

Bob frowned. "We'll have to leave him at Mike's for the time being," he answered. "At least until we know what's happening. Jake's safe enough there."

"But what if the clinic is flooded?"

"It won't be," Carole said. "Not yet, anyway. Neil, you can trust Mike to make sure that Jake's OK. Give him a call if you're really worried."

The phone rang in the office, and she went to answer it. Everyone else went into the kitchen, and Bob put the kettle on. Neil helped himself to a bowl of cereal for a second breakfast.

"That was Bev," said Carole when she reappeared. "She says the floodwater's rising along her street and they've got to leave their house. I told her the whole family could come here."

"Yay!" Sarah cried, jumping up and down. "She'll bring Milly! I love Milly!"

Bev was one of the Parkers' full-time kennel assistants, and her dog, Milly, was a favorite at King Street.

"But she'll also bring that cat," said Neil less enthusiastically.

"She's called Steppy, not *that cat*," said Emily. "And anyway, I'll look after her. You don't have to bother."

"It's settled then," said Carole. "Emily, you'll have to share with Sarah so that Bev can have your room. I'll pull out the sofa bed in the living room for her son, Andrew. Bev's husband is away at the moment, so we don't have to worry about him."

"What about Kate?" Neil asked, remembering the Parkers' other kennel assistant, Kate Paget. "Is she here yet?"

"No, she also called while you were out," said Carole. "She wasn't sure if she could get here. I told her not to bother, but she said she'd try anyway."

"I hope she's OK," said Emily anxiously.

The phone rang again, and Emily jumped up to go and answer it. Carole sat at the kitchen table and sipped the mug of tea Bob had put in front of her. "We've got to get organized," she said. "The phone's been ringing all morning, so I haven't even started the feedings yet. That's the first job."

"Sure is!" said Neil. The usual early morning barking from the kennel blocks sounded louder than ever. The dogs were hungry and not used to being cooped up for so long.

"I could take the dogs into the barn for some exercise," he suggested. "We did it before, remember? During all that snow last winter. It's better than nothing."

"Good idea," said Bob. "Just two or three at a time.

You can get started as soon as they're all fed. It'll give us a chance to clean the pens."

"That was Mrs. Fox," said Emily as she came back into the kitchen. "She says she was supposed to bring her dog in, but she can't get here."

"I remember," said Carole. "A saluki. Beautiful animal. Well, if she can't, she can't. What did you tell her?"

"I just said to let us know if she thought she'd manage it later."

"Good," said Bob. "OK, Emily, you're on phone duty. Take messages, and find one of us if it looks like there's a problem."

"There are a few people who are supposed to be picking up their dogs today," said Carole. "I doubt they'll be able to get here, either."

"OK, everyone," Bob said as he rubbed his hands together, "Let's get moving."

Neil scraped the bottom of his cereal bowl for the last few cornflakes. "King Street forever!" he declared.

Neil spent the morning playing with the dogs in the barn, making sure that they got at least a little bit of the exercise they had missed since the heavy rain began. He would have thoroughly enjoyed himself, especially since he should have been in school, if he hadn't been missing Jake so much. Even though he knew his dog would be well taken care of, he wasn't sure that Jake would be happy without him in an unfamiliar place.

He made one attempt to get ahold of Mike Turner by phone, but only reached his answering machine. The recorded message asked callers to try again later. Neil guessed that Mike was out and about, trying to reach the animals that needed him.

By lunchtime, everything was organized. Bev had arrived — after taking a very roundabout route to King Street through Padsham and Colshaw — with her son, Andrew, Milly, and Steppy the cat. Milly was a cheerful little dog who had lost a leg in an accident but was as active on three legs as most dogs were on four.

Bev and Andrew joined in the job of cleaning out the pens, while Neil made sure Milly and Steppy settled down in the office with Emily. Bob made a huge pot of his famous spaghetti bolognese for lunch, and everybody crowded around the kitchen table for a well-deserved meal.

They were halfway through the main course when there was a knock on the back door and Kate Paget came into the kitchen, followed by her husband, Glen and their white mongrel, Willow.

"Kate!" Carole exclaimed, while Neil left the table to get a towel for Willow. "Thank goodness you made it!"

"I thought we weren't going to," said Kate, peeling off another drenched jacket to add to the collection by the door.

Glen grinned. His long blond hair was plastered to his head, and his jeans were muddy up to the knees. "We tried driving across the field," he explained. "I thought we were going to make it, and then I drove through a puddle that was deeper than it looked. The car broke down, so we had to leave it behind and walk the rest of the way. I hope it doesn't get washed away!"

"It won't. Come on, you must be freezing," said Carole. "Sit down. Warm up. Have something to eat. There's a lot left."

Bob got up to fill two extra plates, while Neil tow-

eled Willow vigorously. The lively little dog, happy in spite of her soaking, swiped her tongue over his face. Milly came up to say hello, too, and Neil fished out dog treats for both of them.

"Dad," he said, "I've been thinking."

"Yes?" said Bob.

"Now that everyone's here, you won't need me this afternoon. I thought I might go over to Old Mill Farm and ask Jane and Richard if I could borrow their boat. Then I could row into Compton and pick up Jake."

Old Mill Farm bordered the Parkers' exercise field and the owners, Jane and Richard Hammond, were good friends of the Parkers. Jane's dog, Delilah, a beautiful Border collie, was Jake's mom.

"Now hang on," Carole said to Neil. "You're not going off in a boat by yourself. It's too dangerous."

"Oh, Mom. . . ." Neil slid into his seat again and attacked the last of his spaghetti. "I'd be really careful," he mumbled with his mouth full.

"No, Neil."

"It's actually not such a bad idea," Bob said. "I'd like us all to be happy if we're going to be here for a few days, and Mike must be finding it hard to look after Jake while doing all his other work. But your mother's right, Neil, you can't go by yourself."

"Will you come with me?" Neil asked.

"There's still a lot of work to be done here," Bob said. "How about you go over there after lunch and check that Jane and Richard are OK? They might appreciate a visit. Then you can ask to borrow the boat. If they agree, maybe one of them will be free to go into Compton with you."

"OK," Neil agreed. He could see that he wasn't likely to get a better deal.

"I'll go, too," said Emily.

"And if Jane and Richard are flooded out," Carole added, "tell them they can come over here. I think we can fit in a few more."

Once lunch was over, Neil and Emily set off across the fields to Old Mill Farm. The rain was heavier than ever, plopping into puddles on the garden path and in the exercise field. Huge clouds shouldered each other across the sky, and almost seemed to be resting on top of the hills, hiding even the highest trees.

Streams of water poured down the sides of the hills, and curtains of rain swept across the field, stinging Neil in the face and forcing him to shut his eyes. Rain was trickling down his neck and also into the tops of his boots.

"It's never going to stop," Emily said.

"It's a good thing we're on a hill," said Neil. "What would happen if we had to move all the dogs out?"

Emily shuddered. "Don't even *think* about it!"

The Hammonds' field that bordered the Parkers' land was empty. As the farmhouse came into view,

Neil and Emily stopped and stared at the scene in front of them.

The millpond had burst its banks and spread over part of the field and the farmyard, though the buildings were still safe. The water in the millstream was churning along, brown and frothy, on its way to the river, and in places the bank had collapsed under the force of the current.

A giant chestnut tree had fallen across the pond and lay with its roots in the air and its branches only a yard or so away from the farmhouse windows.

"Come on!" Neil yelled.

Slipping on the wet grass, they hurried down to the farmhouse. As they drew closer, the front door burst open and Jane Hammond ran out, an old raincoat held over her head against the rain.

"Neil! Emily!" she called. "It's Delilah! She's run away! Have you seen her?"

CHAPTER THREE

"What happened?" Neil asked.

He and Emily met Jane on the gravel parking area in front of Old Mill farm. She looked as if she was going to burst into tears and her voice was panicked. "I let her out for a few minutes," she said, "and then the bank of the stream gave way and the tree fell. Delilah was terrified. She just took off down the lane. I couldn't catch her."

As she spoke, she led the way back to the house, and when they were all inside she slammed the door against the terrible weather outside.

"Delilah didn't come to King Street," Neil said.

Jane pulled off the raincoat and thrust her hands through her dark curls. "I don't know what to do," she said. "I'm so worried."

The door to the living room opened and Richard Hammond came out. "I called the police," he began. "They said — oh, hi, Neil, Emily."

"The police haven't seen her?" Jane asked.

"No." Richard put his arm round his wife's shoulders. "If Delilah was heading for Compton, she hasn't had time to get there yet. I spoke to Sergeant Moorhead and he said he'll make sure everyone keeps an eye out for her. His whole team is already out and about in town, rescuing stranded people and pets."

Jane didn't seem very comforted. "I should never have let her out," she said miserably.

"It's not your fault," Emily said. "You didn't know the tree was going to fall."

Neil could see that Jane was trying hard not to cry. He'd always thought she was a particularly tough person, and he'd never seen her so upset — but he knew how much she cared for Delilah.

"I've got an idea, Jane," Neil said. He explained about Jake and how he and Emily had come over to Old Mill Farm to borrow their boat. "If we go into Compton to fetch Jake," he explained, "we can look for Delilah as well."

Jane looked brighter. "Of course! I'll come with you and help row the boat."

"Take the cell phone with you," Richard added. "If Delilah comes back, or if there's any news, I can let you know."

"Great!" said Neil. "What are we waiting for?"

The Hammonds' rowboat was tied to a post on the bank of the millpond. Neil and Jane had to wade out to it through the flood, and Neil held the boat steady while Jane used a plastic bucket to bail out the rainwater that had collected inside. Emily borrowed Jane's cell phone to call their parents and let them know what was happening.

By the time Jane took the oars and guided the boat into the millstream, she was looking a lot more cheerful. Neil felt better, too, even though the rain was as heavy as ever. He was looking forward to being reunited with Jake.

"Which way are we going?" he asked Jane. "Down to the river? That would take us nearly all the way into the center of town."

"No," she said. "Too dangerous. There's too much water coming down from the hills. It would be really difficult to control the boat. As soon as we can, I'm going to get off the river and row across the fields." Jane was concentrating on keeping the boat steady and avoiding the worst of the floating branches and debris. The current was so fast that she hardly had to row at all, but the churning water was driving the boat in all different directions.

Neil clutched the side of the boat as it lurched and spun sideways with the current before Jane got it under control again. "I see what you mean," he said.

After a few minutes, they came to a place where

the stream had burst its banks. The force of the current slackened, and Jane turned the boat to head across the fields. A sheet of water stretched as far as the eye could see. Only a few trees and the line of a half-submerged hedge showed that they were rowing across fields and not some enormous lake.

"We're on Harry Grey's land," Jane said after a while. "I'm going to head for the farmhouse and see if Delilah went there."

Neil didn't think it was likely. Priorsfield Farm lay closer to the river and some of the farm buildings rose out of a waste of water. Before they reached them, they heard a bark and a voice hailing them. Harry Grey came gliding through the water toward them in a long, narrow boat. Tuff, his Jack Russell terrier, was standing on the flat section at the front, barking eagerly.

"Oh, look!" said Emily, laughing. "Harry's Ark!"

In the body of the boat was a drenched and unhappy-looking sheep, along with half a dozen hens that squawked and fluttered as Harry Grey brought the mini-barge alongside the rowboat.

"Hi, Tuff. Hi, Mr. Grey," said Neil. He patted Tuff, who padded to the edge of the platform to sniff at him. Neil gave him a doggy treat. "Where did you get this boat from? It's great!"

Harry Grey managed a smile. He was a tall, weather-beaten man with gray hair, and at the mo-

ment he looked tired. "I've had it for years. I used to
use it on all the rivers around here when I was a boy."

"This weather's hit you badly, hasn't it?" Jane said.
"Do you need any help?"

Mr. Grey shook his head. "I reckon we can cope. I
shifted all the livestock up into the top field yesterday." He gestured toward higher ground rising out of
the waters beyond the farmhouse. It was dotted with
sheep. "Now I'm just rounding up the stragglers."

"Mr. Grey, has Delilah been here?" Neil asked.

"You've lost Delilah?" Harry Grey listened while
Jane explained how Delilah had panicked when the
tree fell and run away. "No, she hasn't been here.
She'd have to swim to get to us. But I'll let you know
right away if she does show up."

He said good-bye and dug his steering pole vigorously into the water. The flat boat slid away in the direction of the top field, and Jane began rowing again. Almost to herself, she said, "If this water gets much deeper, Harry's going to lose all his animals."

Neil and Emily exchanged an anxious look. Neil had been so worried about Jake that he hadn't really thought about what the flood might mean to the local farmers. They could lose their crops and their animals and there wouldn't be anything they could do about it.

"It's got to stop soon," Emily said, but she didn't sound confident.

Rain was still sweeping across the desolate landscape when they reached the outskirts of Compton. Neil could see that the river had overflowed along its course through the center of town. Jane guided the boat up one of the flooded streets. The water level had almost reached the downstairs windows of the houses, while lampposts, fences, and hedges poked up above the surface. Everything seemed deserted, as if the people who lived there were long gone.

"I wonder where they all went," said Neil.

"Think of the mess when they come back!" Emily added.

The houses were built on the slopes of a gentle hill, so as Jane rowed up the street, the water level gradually dropped. At the next corner, the bottom of the rowboat started to scrape along the ground. Jane jumped out and fastened the rope to the nearest lamppost.

Neil and Emily climbed out after her. Water sloshed over the tops of Neil's boots and trickled down icily to his feet. Leaving the boat, they plodded upward until they weren't splashing in water anymore. Neil realized that Mike Turner's clinic was only a couple of streets away.

When they reached it, the main entrance was locked, but when Neil rang the bell, Janice, Mike Turner's nurse, came and opened it. As Neil stepped inside, there was a swift patter of feet. An excited black-and-white shape appeared through the door from the waiting room and hurled itself at Neil.

"Hey, Jake! Steady, boy!"

Neil staggered back, saved himself from falling, and crouched down so he could hug his dog. Jake was wild with delight at seeing his owner again. When their first greeting was over, Neil pulled back, passed his hands over Jake's glossy fur, and looked into his bright eyes with their lively and intelligent expression.

"He's fine!" he said, with a huge sigh of relief. "He's just fine!"

"Just stay away from the dessert in the future, Jake," Emily said, bending down to pat the Border collie.

Meanwhile, Jane was telling Janice about Delilah.

"We haven't heard anything," Janice said. "But Mike isn't here. I'll tell him when he checks in."

"Where is Mike?" Neil asked.

"The last I heard," Janice said, "he was trying to deliver a calf in two feet of floodwater. But he left a message for you. Just keep Jake's diet plain and simple for the next couple of days, and there shouldn't be any more problems."

"OK, thanks," said Neil.

"Are you staying here?" Jane asked Janice. "Shouldn't you be at home?"

"That's what's worrying me," Janice said. "I'm afraid if I hang around for much longer, I won't be able to *get* home. But there's still another dog, Patti, besides Jake, and I can't leave her. She's well enough to go home, and I've tried calling her owners, but they're not answering their phone."

"You mean they just went off and left her?" Neil asked indignantly.

Janice shrugged. "I don't know. She's really missing them, too. I brought both Patti and Jake into the office with me. I thought Jake would be company for Patti, but she's still down in the dumps."

She led the way into the office. Neil and Emily crowded through the door behind her. On the floor beside Janice's chair was a dog basket, with a silky little King Charles spaniel curled up inside it.

"Hi there, Patti," said Emily.

Patti just raised her head, looked mournfully at them for a minute, and then laid her nose down on her paws again.

"Oh, she's a cutie," said Emily. She squatted down by the basket and stroked Patti's head. "It's all right, girl, we'll find your owners for you."

"We'll take her," said Neil. "We can try her house, and if there's no one there, we'll take her to the rescue center. No problem."

"If you're sure." Janice looked at the rain beating against the window. "I don't think any dog should be out in this."

"She can stay under my coat," said Emily. She picked up the little dog and cradled her in her arms. "I'll look after her."

"Well . . . all right," Janice said. "It's a load off my mind. I was beginning to think I'd be stranded here."

She wrote down the address of Patti's owners, and Jane and the Parkers left, with Patti cuddled inside Emily's jacket and Jake bounding happily at Neil's side.

The rowboat was where they had left it, but the water had risen above their knees when they waded out to it and climbed in. Jake swam part of the way and shook water over everyone when Neil hauled him into the boat.

"Oh, well," Neil said. "We can't get any wetter!"

The house where Patti's owners, the Harpers,

lived was not far away. Neil took the oars to give Jane a rest. It felt weird to be rowing along streets where he had so often walked or ridden his bike.

The floodwater was lapping against the Harpers' front door, just above the level of the doorstep. Neil lay the oars inside the boat and waited while Jane clambered out, waded up the path, and knocked. There was no reply.

"Tap at the window," Neil suggested, and while Jane knocked again, he shouted, "Hey! Anyone at home?" Jake helped by adding a loud bark.

Still no reply. Jane shrugged and sloshed her way back to the boat.

"We'll take her home," Emily said, hugging Patti to her. "She'll be fine with us."

"And when the Harpers *do* turn up," Neil added, "I'll have something to say to them!" He pulled on the oars again, and the boat forged on down the street.

"We'd better go home," Jane said. "It's getting late."

Neil knew why she sounded so despondent. In all their traveling around Compton, they hadn't seen any sign of Delilah.

Their route home took the boat and its band of human and doggy occupants past Meadowbank School. Floodwater covered the playground so that nothing could be seen except the top half of the jungle gym.

Just as he was rowing past the gate, Neil heard barking coming from the school building. "Hey!" he said. "Can you hear that dog?"

Jane began to look hopeful again. Neil stepped out of the boat and sloshed across the playground. As he drew nearer to the school building, a second-floor window was thrown open and his teacher, Mr. Hamley, looked out. The barking came again, louder this time, and the teacher's crazy Dalmatian, Dotty, put her paws up on the windowsill.

"Oh, it's Dotty!" said Neil, laughing. "Do you want to go for a swim?"

Mr. Hamley grabbed Dotty's collar. He was looking pretty stressed out.

"Hello!" he called. "Did you want something?"

"We're looking for Delilah." Neil explained what had happened. "Have you seen her, Mr. Hamley?"

"No, sorry, Neil. I've been here all day with Mrs. Thorn, shifting the files and the equipment off the ground floor. I only brought Dotty because she was going crazy at home."

Behind Neil, Jane looked disappointed. "Paul, will you let me know if you see her?" she shouted up to him.

"Of course I will. Right away," said Mr. Hamley. "No, Dotty! Bad girl!"

Dotty had started scrabbling at the windowsill as if she was going to launch herself into the water below. Mr. Hamley hauled her back into the classroom and slammed the window down again.

Jane rubbed her hands over her face. "Come on, Neil, I'll take over," she said, getting up to change places with him. "We've done all we can."

She sounded even more tired and discouraged. Neil jumped back into the boat, but he couldn't think of anything to say to cheer her up. He hugged Jake to him. He knew how worried he would feel if his dog was lost in the rising floodwater.

The quickest way back to King Street Kennels was to row across the school playing field, then alongside the river back toward Harry Grey's land, and then home.

A belt of trees marked the line of the river. Though Jane kept her distance from them, she had under-estimated the force of the water, and soon Neil could feel a current tugging at the boat, dragging it across the fields and trying to sweep them back toward the town.

Jane fought to keep the boat steady and guide it back into calmer water. Jake put his paws up on the seat in the stern and started barking loudly. Neil clutched his collar, staring down into the brown swirling water, where foam and scraps of debris spun on the surface.

Patti was whimpering and squirming inside Emily's jacket. Emily stroked her head gently to comfort her.

The boat rocked violently as a huge branch matted with weeds and floating debris slammed into it. Jane fended it off with one oar.

Neil leaned over and helped by pushing the branch, but as he did so, he saw a strip of red leather tangled in the weeds. "Hey, stop!" he yelled.

As the branch twisted around, he saw something else lying across it, too — something smooth and brown, with a leg outstretched. Instead of pushing the branch, he now tried to grab it, but the current had carried it out of reach.

"Jane, stop! There's a dog on that branch!"

CHAPTER FOUR

Jane Hammond back-paddled, struggling to maneuver the rowboat close to the branch in the water again. Neil leaned over, but he still couldn't quite reach it. Jake put his paws up on the side of the boat and let out a sharp bark. The boat lurched dangerously.

"Steady," Jane said. "Neil, wait a minute."

Bubbling over with impatience and worry for the dog he'd spotted, Neil sat back in the boat and gave Jane the chance to row it even closer. The current was tugging at both the boat and the clump of debris, so it was hard for her to bring the boat alongside the branch.

"Neil, do you think that dog's dead?" Emily said in a shaky voice.

"I don't know," Neil muttered. His heart beat
fiercely at the thought.

As soon as the branch was within reach again,
Neil leaned over and grabbed it. The clump of debris
clinging to it began to break up, and the shape of the
dog became clearer. It was small and brown. It didn't
move as the trash surrounding it was washed away
and floated free.

Neil stretched over the side of the boat, leaning
dangerously far out, but he couldn't quite get ahold
of the dog. It started to sink.

"No!" Emily sobbed.

As he made a wild grab and missed, Neil heard a
splash and saw that Jake had thrown himself into
the water. He swam over to the small brown dog and
managed to grip its collar between his teeth.

"Jake!" Neil shouted, terrified that his dog would
go under as well. "Jake, get back here!"

Paddling vigorously, Jake headed for the boat, and
within seconds, Neil was able to grab him and haul
him out along with the dog he had rescued.

"Good job, boy!" he said as both Jake and the
strange dog flopped into the bottom of the boat.

"Jake, you're a hero!" Emily added.

Jake grinned a doggy grin and shook himself.

Neil was already examining the other dog. He was
a young chocolate-brown Labrador, smaller than
Jake. His brown fur was plastered to his body by the
water. He lay limp in Neil's hands, as if he was dead.

Neil pinched one of the little dog's paws. Emily let out a cry of delight as she saw his eyelids twitch.

"We'll get him to your dad," Jane said, beginning to row back in the direction of King Street Kennels.

Neil knew that would be too late. If anyone was going to save this dog, it had to be him. He'd seen his father teach a dog owner about reviving dogs, and he knew he had to give it a try. "This dog needs my help now!" he said urgently. He pulled the little dog up and held him upside down, until water trickled out from between his jaws. Then he laid the limp body across his knees and poked a finger into the dog's mouth to bring his tongue forward and clear out some scraps of leaves and grass that were blocking his airway.

Holding the dog's mouth closed, Neil put his own mouth around the dog's nose, and blew. He could feel the dog's chest rise and fall. *Again. Blow. Again,* he repeated in his head.

Neil wasn't aware of the rain anymore or the flood-water and the motion of the boat. His full attention was concentrated on the little dog. He kept blowing steadily into his nose.

Suddenly, Emily cried, "Neil, he's breathing!"

Neil raised his head. The little dog coughed feebly, and more water gushed out of his mouth. His eyes fluttered open and then closed again, but his breathing didn't stop.

"Will he be OK?" Emily asked anxiously. "He must be less than a year old."

Neil grinned. "I hope so."

"Good going, Neil," said Jane.

Neil took off his jacket and used the inside — which was a bit drier than the outside — to gently towel off the dog, and then to wrap him. Patti poked her head out of Emily's coat to watch, while Jake edged up to the dog and sniffed curiously.

Neil rumpled his ears. "You're a hero, Jake, a real lifesaver."

"Is there anything that says who owns him?" Jane asked.

Neil had been too busy to think about that until now. He parted the folds of the jacket until he could see the dog's collar and the tag that hung from it.

"There's a phone number," he said, turning the tag over. "And — hey, you won't believe this! It says his name's Noah!"

He laughed, and Emily joined in. Relief made the name seem much funner than it really was.

"Poor old Noah!" Neil gasped. "You must have lost your ark!"

Jane half-rowed, half-dragged the boat across the flooded fields straight for King Street Kennels and grounded it at the bottom of the hill, not far from the Parkers' exercise field. Everyone piled out.

"I'll leave the boat here," she said as she and Neil tugged it out of the water. "I can walk home from

here, and I don't think I could row back up the millstream against the current."

She tied the rope to a bush and set off with Neil
and Emily for the exercise field gate. Neil broke into
a trot, with Noah bundled in his arms. He knew the
little dog still needed care — and fast — if he was
going to recover.

Emily let Patti down for a run and hurried after
her brother, while Jake bounded alongside.

Neil was panting as he reached the kitchen door
and flung it open. "Mom —" he began, but then
stopped when he saw that the kitchen was crowded.
Along with Bob and Carole, Maude Lumley and her
sister, Val Jennings, were sitting at the table drink-
ing tea. Two of Maude's dogs, Ludo and Spangle,
were sprawled comfortably on the floor, while her
other dog, a tiny Yorkshire terrier called Yap, was
curled up on Sarah's lap.

As Neil and the others came in, Spangle the
spaniel sprang to her feet and started barking enthusiastically.

Neil, despite being soaked through and through,
couldn't help grinning. As usual, Spangle was covered in mud.

Yap sprang up, too, and bounced over to Emily,
while the gentle Labrador, Ludo, just raised her
head as if she was giving them a friendly welcome.

Patti shrank back against Emily as though all

these strange dogs were too much for her, but Jake came boldly into the kitchen to give them all an interested sniff.

"We're flooded out," Val Jennings said.

"We didn't know what to do with the dogs, so we came here. I hope we're not being a nuisance," her sister, Maude, added.

"Of course not," Carole said.

"Mom, Dad. We rescued a dog!" Neil held out Noah, still wrapped in his jacket. "We picked him out of the water."

Bob snapped to attention. He took Noah in his big, gentle hands and laid him down by the oven to examine him carefully. Meanwhile, Emily explained to Carole about Patti.

"Maybe her owners got stranded somewhere," Carole said. "Anyway, she can go in the rescue center for now. Can you take her over there, Emily? Then bring a basket for this little guy. He'll have to stay here till we're sure he's going to be all right."

Emily went out again with Patti.

Jane was standing in the kitchen doorway. "Carole, I don't suppose there's any news of Delilah?" she asked.

Carole shook her hand. "No, I'm really sorry."

Jane forced a smile. "I'd better go home."

She refused Carole's offer of tea and went out. Neil watched her walk away across the courtyard with her head down. It looked like she was crying.

When she had gone, Neil squatted down beside his dad and Noah. "What do you think, Dad? Will he be OK?"

Bob Parker looked up, smiling. "I think he's had a very lucky escape. You did a great job saving him. I'd guess that all he needs now is warmth and rest, but as soon as Mike Turner can get out here, I'll ask him to take a look."

"Great," said Neil. "I'll see if I can get in touch with his owners." He took another look at the phone number on Noah's collar, then went to the office to make the call. The phone at the other end rang, and then an answering machine picked up. Neil left a message reassuring Noah's owners that the little dog was in good hands and telling them to phone King Street.

Just as Neil hung up the phone, it rang again. "Yes?" he said.

"Is Mr. or Mrs. Parker there?" a man's voice asked.

"Hold on." Neil went back to the kitchen. His dad and Emily were settling Noah into a basket, so he spoke to Carole. "Someone's on the phone for you."

"What now?" Carole said, and went out.

Neil grabbed a cookie from the plate on the table and said to Mrs. Lumley, "Are the floods really bad where you are?"

"Dreadful!" the old lady said.

"There's three feet of water in our kitchen," Val Jennings added. "We had to leave. We've managed to get a room in a hotel just up the road from here, but they won't take the dogs."

Maude Lumley smiled down at her three beloved friends. "Your mother's really kind, Neil, to take them all in at short notice like this."

Neil bent down to stroke Ludo's head, and slipped her the last piece of his cookie. "We'd never turn a dog away, Mrs. Lumley. Especially not great dogs like these three!"

Just then, Carole came back into the kitchen. "I never knew a rainstorm could cause so much damage."

"What's the matter?" Neil asked.

"That was the manager of the White Rose Hotel on the phone," Carole replied. "He had to cancel our reservation for the party. He says that the hotel's flooded."

"Oh, no!" Emily said, looking up from where she was stroking Noah.

Sarah's face crumpled as if she was going to cry.

"Won't the water have gone down by then?" Neil said.

"By Saturday?" said Carole. "I doubt it. And even then, think of the mess in their garden!" She sighed and shook her head. "We'll just have to postpone the party, that's all."

"But we've sent out all the invitations," Emily objected.

"Then I'll have to call everyone, I suppose," her mom said. "Neil, can you let Max know?"

"Sure. But just a minute," said Neil. "Why don't we hold the party here, in the barn? You did Kate's wedding reception there, Mom, and it was great!" He grinned at his mom. "That'd be even better than the White Rose Hotel!"

"Well . . . yes." Carole pushed her hair back behind her ears. "It's a good idea, Neil. But I can't possibly get all the food ready in time. I can't even get to the supermarket. Not with everything else I have to do." She sighed again. "No, we'll have it later, when everything is back to normal."

But it won't be on the right day, Neil thought. *It won't be the same.*

CHAPTER FIVE

Water surged all around Neil. He was floundering in it, trying to hold his head up. Somewhere in the flood, Jake was drowning, and Sam was struggling in the current, trying to reach him. Neil thrashed violently as he sank.

Gasping, Neil opened his eyes.

Everything was dark and quiet. Neil was tangled up in his blankets, but lay safe in bed, in his room at King Street.

For just a few minutes, he had dreamed he was reliving the dreadful day when his beloved dog Sam had died in his efforts to save Jake from drowning.

Neil didn't think he would ever forget that day.

He tried to sit up and realized there was an unexpected weight on the bed. He heard a soft whining, and felt the warm rasp of a tongue over his face.

"Jake," he said softly. "You silly dog!" He put out an arm and drew his dog's warm body tight against him.

Jake wriggled and licked him again, and Neil had to stifle his laughter so that he wouldn't disturb the rest of the house.

Then he remembered Delilah and didn't feel like laughing anymore.

"We'll find your mom tomorrow, Jake," he whispered. "We've got to get her back. For Jane's sake."

When Neil came down for breakfast the next morning, the kitchen was crowded. Bev and her son, Andrew, were sitting at the table with the rest of the Parkers. Bev's dog, Milly, gave an excited bark as Jake followed Neil in, and the two dogs rolled over happily together.

Neil only had eyes for Noah, sitting up in his basket beside the stove. "Hi there, Noah!" he said, crouching down so that he could make friends with him.

Now that the little dog was recovering his spirit, Neil could see that Noah's coat was sleek and shiny — and his eyes bright. The dog let out a high-pitched bark as Neil bent down beside him, and he thumped his stumpy tail up and down.

"He's a great little dog," Bob Parker said, looking

down from where he stood at the stove, grilling bacon.

"I love him," said Sarah. "I want him to stay here forever and ever."

Neil groaned and Emily rolled her eyes. Sarah wanted *every* dog who came to King Street to stay there forever and ever.

"He's been well taken care of," Bob said. "Somebody must be looking for him."

"I'd be frantic if he was mine," Carole said.

Neil was just taking his place at the table when

the phone rang. "Maybe that's Noah's owners now," he said, getting up again. "I left a message."

When Neil picked up the phone, a woman's voice spoke. "You're the people who look after stray dogs, aren't you? Well, there's one on my garage roof."

Neil was still thinking about Noah, and wondered if he'd heard right. "It's *where*?"

"On my garage roof. There's water all around it. Can you do anything?"

"Can't the fire department help?" said Neil, thinking practically.

"Everyone seems to be busy," said the woman.

"Hold on, I'll tell my dad," Neil said. Then an idea struck him, and he added, "What does it look like?"

"The dog? Um, I'm not sure," the woman said. "I think it's black and white."

"What breed?" Neil asked, thinking it might be Delilah. Excitement surged over him.

"I'm sorry, it's just a dog to me. Can you get here soon?"

"Yes, of course." Neil wrote down her name and address on a notepad. "We'll be right over!" he promised, and hung up the phone.

Dashing into the kitchen, he announced, "I think I've found Delilah!"

Emily looked up from her cereal. "That's great! Where?"

Neil waved the paper he had torn off the pad and

explained about the stray dog. "It must be Delilah. I'm going to tell Jane."

"Eat your breakfast first," Carole said. "I'll call Jane in a minute, and then we'll decide what to do."

Neil sat down and started to shovel in his breakfast, managing to slip a scrap of bacon now and then to Jake under the table. Carole finished the last of her toast and went out into the hall.

She was smiling when she came back. "Jane's really hopeful," she said. "She's going to pick Delilah up now. I said you'd meet her at the boat and give her a hand."

"Me, too," said Emily, gulping down her orange juice as she got up from the table.

Jake barked loudly and bounced across the room to Neil. "OK, buddy," Neil said, ruffling his ears. "Let's go and rescue your mom."

Neil crouched in the boat with his shoulders hunched against the driving rain and his parka hood pulled up. On the opposite seat, Emily was huddled into her raincoat as well, but she was smiling, and so was Jane, who had taken the oars. Jake was sitting beside Neil, bright-eyed with anticipation. Everyone was excited at the thought of seeing Delilah again.

The floods had risen even higher since the day before. Most of High Street was under water. At the deepest end, in Compton's Market Square, the railings around Queen Victoria's statue poked up above the surface like spear points. Neil thought the queen looked even more disapproving than usual as she gazed down at the swirling water.

Jane guided the boat carefully across the square and past the town hall. Floodwater was lapping over the top of the steps and around the bases of the columns that held up the roof of the entrance porch. All the windows were tightly shut.

As a small whirlpool drove the boat closer to the building, Jake sprang to his feet and let out a sharp bark. Neil reached out to lay a hand on his dog's wet fur.

"Steady, Jake," he said. "It's OK."

But Jake didn't seem to be paying attention. He was staring up at the roof of the town hall, whining softly.

"What is it, boy?" said Neil.

He looked up, trying to see what had startled Jake, but there was nothing in sight except for the gables and decorated spires that made up the roof of the building, with the clock in the center.

"There's nothing there," said Emily.

Jake sat down by Neil's feet again, but he kept his eyes fixed on the town hall roof as the boat gradually pulled away.

Jane rowed on, along High Street toward the park. All the shops were closed, and most of them had shutters over their windows. A church parking lot looked like a swimming pool, but the church itself was still completely above water. Neil could see lights on inside.

Mrs. Dixon, the woman who had called, lived near the park, not far away from Bev's house. As the boat turned into her road, Neil could see that the houses were safely above the water, but the garages, slightly lower down, were surrounded.

"There she is!" Emily cried excitedly as the boat drew nearer to Mrs. Dixon's house and they all caught sight of a Border collie padding up and down the edge of the roof, looking into the water.

Neil was about to cheer.

Then Jane said, "No. That's not Delilah."

CHAPTER SIX

"**B**ut it must be Delilah!" said Emily, dismayed. "It's just got to be!"

Neil peered through the drizzle at the dog. He couldn't make it out clearly, but it looked bigger than Delilah. And he knew Jane would recognize her own dog, just as he would recognize Jake.

He turned his head at the sound of a window opening, and a woman poked her head out. "Hello!" she called. "Are you the Parkers?"

"Yes!" Neil yelled back. "We've come to get the dog."

"Good! The poor thing must be terrified." Mrs. Dixon went on watching anxiously as Jane tried to maneuver the rowboat up to the garage. Before they could reach it, the boat nudged against the hard road surface underneath.

Jane was resting on her oars, looking tired and frustrated.

"Maybe the dog can get to us?" Emily said hopefully.

"Here, boy!" Neil called.

Jake added a high-pitched bark. The marooned dog stood on the edge of the roof, let out a couple of barks in reply, and plunged into the water.

But instead of swimming toward the boat, it struck out strongly in the opposite direction, toward the house.

"No — this way!" Neil shouted.

The dog scrambled onto the doorstep. It shook itself vigorously, gave one last look at Neil and the others in the boat, and vanished through the hedge into the garden next door.

"Well!" Mrs. Dixon exclaimed from her window. "Would you believe it!"

"He wasn't stranded at all," said Neil.

"But will he be all right?" Emily asked. "Maybe we should try to catch him. People who are looking out for Delilah may think it's her and call us."

Jane started to row along the street again in the direction the dog had disappeared. Neil gave Mrs. Dixon a wave as she closed her window, then tried to catch another glimpse of the mysterious dog among the bushes in the next garden. There was no sign of it.

"What should we do?" said Emily.

"There's not much we can do," Jane said. "He's faster than us, in the boat or on foot. He obviously doesn't want to be rescued."

"He's a good swimmer," said Neil. He hated the thought of abandoning any dog, but he had to admit that this dog didn't seem to need him.

As Jane began to row more quickly back the way they had come, Neil kept his eyes peeled, but the Border collie didn't appear again.

Their immediate hopes of rescuing Delilah had vanished. Neil knew there was nothing to do but go home. He rumpled Jake's wet fur. "Never mind, boy," he said. "We'll find your mom somehow." But he was finding it hard to believe.

As they rowed past the church again, Neil could see that the lights were still on. "Why don't we stop here?" he suggested. "There might be somebody who knows something."

Jane didn't look very hopeful, but she guided the boat up to the gate and tied it to the post.

Neil led the way as they plodded up the raised path to the church. Even Jake walked with his head down, as if he had lost most of his energy.

The outer doors of the church stood open. When Neil pushed open the inner doors, warmth and light greeted him, along with the sound of voices and someone playing a guitar.

"Hello," said a voice. "You look soaking wet. Would you like some tea?"

Neil turned to see Gavin Thorpe, the judge of Compton. He was presiding over a huge tea kettle set on a trestle table at the back of the church. His black Labrador, Jet, was lying beside him, and gently thumped his tail against the floor as Jake went up to sniff him.

"Tea would be great, thanks, Gavin," said Jane, slapping her hands together to get them warm.

While Gavin filled three mugs with tea, Neil looked around the church. He recognized the guitar player as Beth Ward, the big sister of one of his friends at Meadowbank School. She was sitting on the steps at the other end of the church with a crowd

of small children around her. Her dog, Denny, was ly-ing beside her with his head cocked, as if he was lis-tening to the music, too.

Closer to Neil, one of the side aisles was spread with sleeping bags and blankets. Two of Neil and Emily's other school friends, Hasheem Lindon and Julie Baker, were sitting there with their heads bent over an electronic game.

Neil took his mug of tea and strolled over to them. "Hi. How's it going?"

"Neil!" Julie scrambled to her feet. "You're not flooded out as well?"

"No, King Street is high and dry. We're looking for a dog." Neil explained about Delilah, but both Julie and Hasheem shook their heads.

"We've been here since last night," Julie said. "We didn't notice any stray dogs. It was bad enough get-ting Ben here."

She pointed to a nearby pew, where her parents were sitting with their big, shaggy Old English sheepdog, Ben, who was fast asleep.

Julie rushed off to talk to Emily, and Hasheem put the game to one side. "Come on," he said to Neil. "Let's take a walk around the church. We've got half the dogs in Compton here."

And we've got the other half, Neil thought as he fol-lowed Hasheem down the aisle. *But not Delilah.*

In the next fifteen minutes, Neil talked to Mrs. Fitz, the Bakers' next-door neighbor, who was cuddling her miniature poodle, Sheba. Also to Mrs. Smedley from the newsstand; Bill Grey, the local butcher, whose huge Irish wolfhound, Fred, took up almost a whole pew to himself; and Eddie Thomas, the local builder, with his wife, Maureen, and their dog, Blackie. Everybody had a story to tell about finding refuge in the church as the floodwaters rose, but no one had seen a dog who might have been Delilah.

Neil reached the back of the church again to find Jane still talking to Gavin Thorpe.

"I don't know what else to do," she was saying. "It's next to impossible to get around in this weather and look for her, and the longer she's missing, the more likely it is . . ."

She broke off, unable to finish what she was saying. Neil silently finished the sentence for her: *The more likely it is she'll have drowned.*

Neil and Jake were following Jane and Emily down the path to where they had left their boat when another boat appeared in the gateway. Neil didn't know the oarsman, but he recognized the man with him — Jake Fielding, the young reporter from the *Compton News*. He wore a flapping leather coat over his usual denim jacket and jeans, and his camera was at the ready.

He jumped out of his boat as the oarsman guided it alongside Jane's. "Hi!" he called. "How are you?"

"Wet," said Neil.

Jake's long hair was soaked and dripping, but he had a broad grin on his face. "I've got some great pictures," he said, patting his camera. "How are your parents coping, Neil?"

"We're not flooded out yet," Neil said, "but it's harder doing the work in all this rain."

"And we've got a lot of extra dogs to look after," Emily added.

Jake, the dog, let out a bark, as if he approved of that.

"Jane," Neil said, "tell Jake about Delilah. He might be able to help."

Jane Hammond was looking depressed, as if she had almost given up hope that anybody could help her find Delilah. But she told the story of what had happened the day before, and how they had searched for Delilah ever since without success.

"Hey, maybe I *can* help," Jake Fielding said. "We just passed Sergeant Moorhead in a boat, and he had a Border collie with him."

Jane's eyes widened. "Was it Delilah?"

The young reporter shook his head. "I'm not sure. I don't know Delilah all that well. But it was definitely a Border collie."

"All right!" said Neil, clambering back into Jane's boat. "Let's go and see! What are we waiting for?"

"Where did you see Sergeant Moorhead?" Jane asked, while Emily and Jake the dog climbed into the boat after Neil.

"Just up the street." Jake pointed back in the direction of the market square. "He looked as if he was on his way to the police station."

Jane took the oars again, and they said good-bye to Jake Fielding, who set off up the path to the church.

"It's got to be Delilah *this* time," Emily said as they headed toward the square.

Neil wasn't so sure, but he started to hope again. Sergeant Moorhead was in charge of Compton's police force. He loved dogs, especially his own German shepherd, Sherlock. Neil knew that the sergeant would do all he could to help reunite Delilah with her owner.

When they reached the market square, it was deserted, and Jane turned down the street that led to the police station. The water level dropped as the road sloped upward, but it was still just about deep enough for the boat. Neil couldn't help thinking again how weird it was to see the street looking like a river, with lampposts and bus stops poking out of it.

Not far along the street, he heard the sound of an engine, and a moment later a small speedboat, powered by an outboard motor, appeared behind them, heading up from the market square. Sergeant Moorhead was standing up in it, with his police dog, Sherlock, at his side, and another policeman at the boat's wheel.

Neil waved both arms over his head. "Hi! Sergeant Moorhead!"

The police sergeant turned and waved at him, then said something to his companion. The speedboat came around in a wide curve and slid gently alongside the rowboat. Neil leaned over to pat Sherlock. While Jake and the big, gentle police dog said hello to each other, Neil quickly scanned inside the boat and exchanged a dismayed glance with Emily. There was no Border collie on board.

"Hello, Neil," the sergeant said. "What can I do for you?"

"We just saw Jake Fielding," Neil explained. "He said you had a Border collie with you."

"We thought it might be Delilah," Jane added.

A look of exasperation crossed Sergeant Moorhead's face. "I did have a Border collie, yes," he said. "But I'm sorry, Mrs. Hammond, it wasn't your Delilah."

Jane sagged wearily over the oars. "I thought it was too good to be true."

"Try not to worry," Sergeant Moorhead said kindly. "I got your report that Delilah was missing, and everybody's keeping a lookout for her. "She'll turn up, I'm sure she will. It's amazing how resilient dogs are. We've found some brave little mutts in the strangest places."

"What about the Border collie you had?" Neil asked.

Sergeant Moorhead snorted. "It was running around in a garden not far from the park," he said. "It took a lot to catch it, I can tell you that. Then when I got it into the boat and set off back to the station, it jumped overboard while my back was turned."

"I bet that's the dog we saw!" said Emily.

Neil laughed. "It must be! Where did it go then?" he asked the sergeant.

"Your guess is as good as mine," Sergeant Moorhead replied. "It swam off up Meadow Lane, just behind the library, and that's the last I saw of it."

"I hope it'll be all right," Emily said anxiously.

"If it's the dog we saw earlier, it's a strong swimmer," said Neil.

"It was heading for the railway station, and there's higher ground up there," said Sergeant Moorhead. "I think that crazy animal was enjoying itself. And what really annoys me is that I didn't get a chance to look at its collar, so I can't even let the owner know."

"Why don't we go up there?" Neil suggested. "We could look for Delilah at the same time."

"Thanks," said the sergeant. "I've got enough to worry about without trying to catch dogs that don't want to be caught."

"OK." Jane sighed and took hold of the oars again. "It can't hurt to try."

"Let me row for a while," said Neil.

While he changed places with Jane, Sergeant Moorhead said good-bye. "Don't worry about Delilah," he said to Jane. "We'll get her back. You'll see." He saluted, and the speedboat pulled away again.

Neil dug the oars determinedly into the water. He could see from Jane's face that she didn't quite believe Sergeant Moorhead's reassurances.

CHAPTER SEVEN

As they rowed toward Compton railway station, Neil and Emily both kept a lookout for Delilah and the mysterious swimming dog. Jane Hammond sat with her shoulders slumped and her elbows on her knees, as if she had given up hope. Neil couldn't think of anything to say to cheer her up.

The rain had started to slacken off. Instead of a downpour, it had become an icy drizzle that was running down the neck of Neil's parka and into his boots. He couldn't remember ever being so wet and cold, and his back had started to ache, so it was hard to keep up the steady rhythm of rowing.

They soon reached the edge of the floods and were able to leave the boat tied to a bus stop sign. Jane decided to stay close by it and search the side streets for Delilah, while Neil and Emily, with Jake at their heels, went on to the train station to investigate.

Neil strode past the ticket counters to the turnstile in front of the platform. A ticket inspector was there, lounging in a little glass booth.

"Have you seen a dog come through here?" Neil asked.

The inspector shook his head. "Can't say that I noticed. What did it look like?"

"A little like this," Neil said, pointing to Jake, who was standing beside him.

"Of course!" the inspector said. He raised his voice to shout along the platform. "Jim! Hey, Jim!"

Neil's heart sank. He suddenly realized who he was going to see. He knew he was right when a small, plump man in overalls appeared at the turnstile. A Border collie was trotting at his heels. Neil recognized the man as Jim Brewster, a railway signalman. His dog, Skip, was Sam's brother and Jake's uncle.

"What's up?" Jim asked. "Oh, hello, Neil. Nice to see you."

"This boy here was asking about your dog," said the ticket inspector.

"Skip?" Jim Brewster smiled and bent down to pat his dog, and Skip looked up at him eagerly. "He's had me on a wild-goose chase."

Neil looked at Skip more closely. His coat was damp and sticking out in all directions, as if he had just had a thorough toweling.

"He wasn't missing, too, was he?" Neil asked.

Jim Brewster looked surprised. "Yes, he was. He ran off this morning when I let him out, first thing."

"Did you tell the police?"

"No, I figured I'd wait a bit. Skip's been off on his own once or twice before, and he always finds his own way home. And Sergeant Moorhead has enough on his plate just now."

"Weren't you worried?" Neil asked. "Because of the floods?"

Chuckling, Jim Brewster shook his head. "No, Skip loves water. He'd swim all day and every day if I let him."

Neil couldn't help grinning, too, even though he was still very worried about Delilah. At least, he thought, he was pretty sure that they'd solved the mystery of the swimming dog. It had been Skip.

"Well, boy," he said, ruffling the dog's damp fur, "you stay on dry land from now on. You're a Border collie, not a mermaid!"

When Neil and Emily returned to the boat, Jane Hammond was waiting for them. She looked even more depressed, and it was obvious she hadn't found any clues as to where Delilah could be. She got back into the boat and took the oars without a word. When everyone else was on board, she headed for home.

Eventually, they came to the place at the bottom of the hill where they had left the boat after their previous expedition. Neil and Jane hauled the boat up out of the water.

"Hey!" Neil said, with the rope in his hands. "That's where we docked before." He pointed to a gorse bush a few yards away from the edge of the water. "The floods are going down!"

"Then why is it still raining?" Emily asked, hunching her shoulders against the cold drizzle.

Neil found another bush, closer to the water. While

he was tying up the boat, Jane said a quick good-bye and walked off in the direction of Old Mill Farm.

Emily watched her go. "She looks really sad," she said.

"I wish there was more we could do," Neil agreed gloomily. "But Delilah could be anywhere."

They set off for home. Jake bounded ahead, splashing through the puddles along the path. They crossed the exercise field and walked up the garden path to the courtyard just in time to see a tall, gray-haired woman coming out of the rescue center with Carole Parker beside her. The woman was carrying Patti, the King Charles spaniel Neil and Emily had brought from Mike Turner's.

Neil exchanged a glance with Emily. "That must be Mrs. Harper," he muttered. "I wonder what her excuse is for leaving Patti."

As they came closer, he was able to hear what Mrs. Harper was saying to his mom.

"I've been out of my mind with worry. We went over to Colshaw to visit my mother, and with the weather being so bad, we decided to stay overnight. Then the next morning we tried to get home, because we had to pick up Patti, and the car broke down. We were marooned — we couldn't even get to a phone!"

Carole murmured something sympathetically. Neil could tell from the way she hugged Patti, and the way that Patti was excitedly licking her face, that dog and owner really loved each other.

"Then, when we finally managed to get in touch with Mike Turner," Mrs. Harper went on, "he told us that Patti was with you. I can't tell you how grateful I am."

"All part of the service," said Carole. "We're just glad to see you back together again."

Mrs. Harper tucked Patti under one arm so she could shake hands with Carole. "I can't thank you enough," she repeated. "Just as soon as we can go home again, I'll put a check in the mail for the rescue center. I insist on making a donation."

Carole thanked her, and Mrs. Harper carried Patti out through the gate to the driveway. A moment later Neil heard a car start up.

"Hi, Mom," he said. "You've got Patti straightened out, then?"

"Yes," she said. Carole was looking tired, but she smiled. "It makes it all worthwhile when you can bring a dog and her owner back together again. Mrs. Harper thinks that the water is low enough now in her part of town for her to drive home." Carole stooped over to greet Jake, who had bounded over to her and was wiping his muddy front paws on her jeans.

"Well, avoid Market Square," said Neil. "It's like the lost city of Atlantis down there."

Carole led the way back to the house. "Neil, would you clean out Patti's pen later so that we can put Noah in there? He's well enough to leave the house now."

"Great!" said Neil.

The kitchen felt wonderfully warm after the cold rain outside. Bob Parker was standing by the oven, stirring a huge pot that sent out enticing smells. Neil and Emily peeled off their wet things while Carole put on the kettle for hot drinks.

Sarah was sitting on the floor, playing with Noah and Milly. "Noah's a very smart dog," she informed the others. "Watch. Sit, Noah, sit!"

The little brown dog sat immediately and looked alertly at Sarah. His stumpy tail drummed on the floor. Neil could see that he'd made a good recovery from his near drowning.

Fishing in his pocket, he pulled out a dog treat and gave it to Noah. Jake, with Milly just behind him, came and nosed at his hand, as if to say, "What about us?"

"OK, OK," Neil said, passing around tidbits. "I haven't forgotten you."

He went to get a towel for Jake, and on his way back to the kitchen, he heard the front doorbell ring. He quickly tossed the towel to Emily and went to answer it.

Standing on the front step was James Harding. He was a friend of the Parkers now, although when he and Neil first met, he had been involved with a gang of antiques robbers and had ended up in prison. When he came out, he got married and set up a business as a dog trainer. It had taken Bob and Carole some time before they could trust him, but he really seemed to be putting the past behind him.

"Hi, Mr. Harding," Neil said as he opened the door. "Are you —"

He stopped and gaped as he took in the scene in front of him. Sitting on the step to one side of Mr. Harding was his dog Jessie, a golden-brown Airedale mix. She was one of the most well-trained dogs Neil had ever met, and the best possible advertisement for Mr. Harding's business.

On his other side was an athletic-looking German shepherd dog, Oliver, who was living with Mr. Harding while being trained for police work. But that wasn't what made Neil stand with his mouth open. It was the other animals.

Mr. Harding was carrying a birdcage with a parrot inside it, and a small black kitten was peering out from his jacket. Neil could see two other dogs in his car, parked at the bottom of the steps.

"They're not all yours, are they?" Neil gasped.

"No." Mr. Harding smiled and shook his head. "They're refugees, Neil. May I have a word with your mom and dad?"

Neil almost asked him to come in, but then he thought of the effect the other animals — especially the kitten — would have in a kitchen where there were already five dogs.

"You'd better go around to the office," he said. "I'll tell Mom and Dad."

Mr. Harding went around to the office door, and Neil called his parents. Bob gave the pot on the stove a final stir and went to see Mr. Harding, while Emily joined Neil.

"What's going on?" she asked.

Neil grinned at her. "Come and see."

In the office, James Harding was just settling into a chair. Jessie sat at his feet, while Oliver remained standing by the door, as if he was on guard. He was a magnificent dog, strongly muscled and intelligent-looking.

"I'm surprised to see Oliver here," said Bob, sitting behind the desk. "Isn't he afraid of water?"

"Not anymore," Mr. Harding said with a proud smile. "We got over all that, didn't we, boy?"

Oliver barked as if he was agreeing.

It had been Mr. Harding's job to train Oliver to overcome his fear of water. It was only this small problem that had stopped Oliver from becoming Compton's new police dog, instead of Sherlock.

"All right!" said Neil, running his hands over Oliver's glossy black-and-tan coat. "Way to go, boy."

"Yes, he's going to join the Colshaw police force next week," said Mr. Harding. "I'll be sorry to see him go, but I think he'll do really well."

"I'm sure he will," said Bob. "So, James, what can we do for you?"

"Well," Mr. Harding began, "I've been running . . . I suppose you'd call it a pet rescue service. Yesterday, one of Barbara's friends called us and said she had to evacuate her house, but she couldn't find her cat. She had to leave it. I said I'd look for it, so I borrowed a boat and I found the cat, up a tree farther down the road. While I was on the way home, I came across a stray dog, stuck on the top of some kid's slide in a backyard. And after that . . . one thing led to another. You'd be surprised how many people were stranded away from home and couldn't get back to look after their pets. Now I've got the original cat and two more, three extra dogs, two rabbit hutches with rabbits, and more gerbils than I want to count."

"And . . ." said Bob, starting to smile.

"And we're full," Mr. Harding said worriedly, running a hand through his hair. "I can't ask Barbara to look after any more. I wondered if you would take these . . . and two more dogs out in the car," he added.

"Yes!" said Neil eagerly.

Bob was laughing. "We'll fit the dogs in," he promised, "and the parrot won't be a problem. I'm not sure about the kitten, though."

"I'll look after her!" Emily said instantly.

She held her hands out, and James Harding gave her the black kitten. The tiny creature sank needle-like claws into her sweater and climbed up to her shoulder, purring loudly. Emily stroked it with a delighted smile on her face. Neil never could understand what his sister saw in cats.

"That looks as if it's settled," said Bob.

"It's a great relief," said Mr. Harding. "I'll go and get the dogs."

As he got to his feet, Neil said, "Mr. Harding, you haven't found a Border collie, have you?"

"A Border collie? No, Neil, I haven't."

Disappointed, Neil explained about Delilah.

"That sounds bad," said Mr. Harding. "I can see why your friend would be worried. I'll do what I can, though. Just as soon as I've settled in these dogs, I'll get back on the job, and I'll keep a special lookout for Delilah."

CHAPTER EIGHT

Neil couldn't remember a morning like the next one at King Street Kennels. On Wednesday, the kitchen seemed as if it would burst. Bev and Andrew were still staying, though Kate had managed to get home the night before to rescue her stranded car. Meadowbank School was still closed, too, because some of the ground-floor classrooms were flood-damaged.

The black kitten and Bev's cat, Steppy, stalked each other in and out of the table legs, while Milly and Jake wrestled together happily on the floor. Sarah could hardly bear to sit still in her chair to eat her breakfast, because she wanted to cuddle all the animals at once. The parrot, in its cage on top of the kitchen cabinets, drowned out all the other noises with earsplitting squawks.

After breakfast, Neil was glad to escape to help with the kennel work. When he went out into the courtyard, he saw that the heavy rain of the last few days had eased off a little. A wind had risen, driving the gray clouds across the sky. Gusts of it slapped rain into Neil's face and rippled the puddles in the courtyard.

Neil pulled up the hood of his parka and ran across to the storeroom, followed by Emily, with Jake bounding alongside. Kate had arrived, and was making up the morning feeds.

"Hi," she said, smiling as they came in. "Guess what? The floods are going down! I saw Sergeant Moorhead on my way here, and he thinks the main road into Compton will be open again by this afternoon."

"Great!" said Neil. "But still no school. Yippee!"

"He didn't have any news of Delilah?" Emily asked.

Kate shook her head. "No. I just hope something awful hasn't happened. Poor Jane. She must be worried sick."

She went on spooning dog food into bowls.

"Need any help?" Neil asked, trying not to think about Delilah.

"You can take these." Kate thrust two bowls into his hands and gave more to Emily. "They're all for Kennel Block Two. They're the last."

They went out again and hurried over to Kennel

Block Two. In the doorway, they met Bev, who was leaving with two of the boarding dogs, a German shepherd and a Labrador. The dogs were pulling on their leashes eagerly, but Bev had them under control.

"You're taking them out?" Neil asked.

"Yes, just as far as the exercise field," said Bev. "I don't think this much rain will bother these big fellows, and they'll be chewing their way out of the pens if they're kept cooped up much longer!"

"Can we give you a hand?" Emily asked.

"The other dogs in here are still eating," Bev said. "But you could go over to your dad in the rescue center and see if he wants any of the dogs there taken out for some exercise."

After Neil and Emily had delivered the bowls of food, they made another dash across to the rescue center.

They found Bob there, stroking his beard as he looked thoughtfully down at one of the dogs James Harding had left the night before.

Neil looked into the pen. The dog, a beautiful Rough collie, was lying in the pen with his nose on his paws and his eyes half-closed. His bowls of food and water were untouched, and when Neil crouched down, snapped his fingers, and said, "Hey, boy!" the dog scarcely blinked.

"Something's not right with him," Bob said.

"You think he's ill?" Neil asked, concerned.

"I don't know. He may just be pining for his owner — but better safe than sorry. Will you go and give Mike a call, and ask him to come out as soon as he can?"

"Sure," said Neil.

"And meanwhile," said Bob, "I'll move him over into the dog clinic. If he's got a cold or virus, I don't want the other dogs catching it."

"At least Noah's OK," Emily said.

She had crouched down in front of the perky little dog, who was now installed in another pen. Noah looked bright and active, rearing up with his paws on the wire mesh while his tail wagged vigorously back and forth.

"He's raring to go!" Neil said, slipping him a dog treat. "I just hope his owners turn up soon."

He went into the office to find Carole already on the phone.

"Thanks for understanding," she was saying. "I hope we'll see you next week. Good-bye." She put the phone down and swiveled the office chair so she was facing Neil. "I've just been making calls to cancel your dad's obedience class tonight," she said. "Half the people won't be able to get here."

"I guess not," said Neil.

"And what can I do for you?" his mother asked him.

Neil explained why he had to call Mike Turner.

"That's all we need!" Carole ran her hands

through her hair and picked up the phone again to dial Mike Turner's number. She got the answering machine and left a message. "I've been thinking about our party," she said when she had finished. "It might not be too late. If everything here is under control, I'm going to contact a few hotels and see if I can find somewhere else to hold it."

"Great!"

"Don't get your hopes up, though," Carole said as she pulled out the phone book. "If I don't manage to do it, I'll have to call all the guests and tell them it's canceled."

She was flipping through the phone book when the front doorbell rang.

"I'll get it," Neil said.

He opened the door to see a young couple standing on the steps. Neil had never seen them before. The man was tall, with close-cropped blond hair, and the woman was smaller, with dark hair. They both wore identical white bomber jackets and black jeans. A white van was parked behind them in the driveway.

"Hi," Neil said. "May I help you?"

"Hi," the man said. "I'm Greg Forrester, and this is my wife, Joanne. We think you might have our dog."

"There was a message on our answering machine," Joanne added.

Neil felt a huge grin spreading over his face. "Hey, you're not Noah's owners, are you?"

"I'm so relieved he's OK!" said Joanne.

"We were away, working," Greg explained. "We run our own business. Our next-door neighbor was looking after Noah, but she was flooded out and had to leave."

"She finally got ahold of us on our cell phone yesterday," Joanne went on, "to tell us that Noah had run off. We came right back to Compton, and when we got home, we found your message."

While they were talking, Neil led the way through the side gate to the rescue center. Bob had just come back from settling the Rough collie into the dog clinic, while Emily had gone into Noah's pen. The little dog was scrambling all over her.

When Neil came in with Joanne and Greg, Noah leaped to the ground and hurled himself at the wire mesh, letting out a stream of excited barks. Joanne crouched down to pet him.

"I can tell he's yours," Neil said, grinning.

Emily scooped up Noah, and brought him out of the pen. Joanne lifted the dog from Emily's arms and hugged him close. Noah covered her face with affectionate licks.

"Where did you find him?" Greg asked.

Bob told the story of how Jake had rescued Noah from the floods and how Neil had revived him and brought him home.

Neil felt embarrassed, especially when he saw that Joanne was nearly crying and holding Noah more tightly than ever.

"I don't know how to thank you," she said. "There must be something we can do."

"Sometimes owners make a donation to the rescue center," Bob said. "But it isn't necessary. Let's go to the office and straighten out this little pup's paperwork."

Everybody trooped back to the house and into the office. Carole was just hanging up the phone, with a frustrated expression on her face.

"No good," she said to Neil, before she saw who was with him. "Everywhere says it's too short notice to hold a big party. The only people who would do it for us say they won't have dogs in the hotel at any price."

"Nevermind, Mom," said Neil. "Look, here are Noah's owners."

A smile spread over Carole's face, wiping away the frustrated look. "Now *that* is good news."

She started to thumb through her files to find Noah's records.

"What's all this about a party?" Greg asked. "Is there a problem?"

"We were going to celebrate our anniversary at the White Rose Hotel this Saturday," said Bob. "But they've been flooded out. I'm afraid we'll have to postpone it."

Greg and Joanne exchanged a glance. Neil couldn't figure out why they were looking so pleased.

"But that's what *we* do," said Greg. "Our business is party catering." He turned around so Neil could see for the first time that there was a logo on the back of his white jacket, and the words *Forrest Feasts*. "If you've got a place to hold the party, we'll provide the food."

"Cool, Mom!" Neil exclaimed. "We can hold it in the barn."

Carole looked at Bob. "What do you think?"

Bob was smiling. "I think we should go for it."

"It'll be *better* in Red's Barn than in some fancy schmancy hotel," said Emily.

"But are you very expensive?" Carole asked, practical as always.

"Mrs. Parker, we wouldn't dream of charging you

anything," Joanne said. "If it wasn't for your son, our dog would be dead."

"Oh, no," said Carole, "we couldn't possibly —"

"I know what we'll do," said Greg. "You pay us what you can afford, and we'll give it to the rescue center. That way everybody's happy."

Neil saw his mother start to smile. "Yes!" he said as Noah let out a delighted bark.

Lunch was nearly as chaotic as breakfast, with everyone swapping the sample menus that Greg and Joanne had left with them. When the meal was over, Neil and Emily slipped out, intending to go over to the barn and plan how to decorate it for the party.

As they crossed the courtyard, the outside gate opened and Maude Lumley came in with her sister, Val. They were both dressed for the weather in boots and raincoats.

"Hello there," said Val. "Now that the weather's clearing up, we thought we'd come over and give our dogs a good walk. Your poor mother must be exhausted."

"Sort of," said Neil, grinning. "Come on, I'll show you where they are."

He led the two sisters over to Kennel Block One, where Ludo and Yap were sharing a pen, while Spangle had the one next door. All three dogs leaped up and started wagging their tails when they saw their owners. Spangle pawed impatiently at the mesh, as if she couldn't wait to get out.

"They look wonderful!" said Maude. "And I've missed them so much."

"I heard the water's going down," said Neil. "You'll be able to go home soon."

Val Jennings shuddered. "Just think of the mess!"

Neil opened up Spangle's pen, fended off the excited spaniel as she shot out, and managed to clip on her leash and give it to Maude. Although the old lady smiled as she greeted her dog, he couldn't help thinking that she looked worried.

"Is anything the matter?" he asked.

"No — well, not really," Maude replied. "It's just that we left the house so quickly, I forgot to take my photo album. It's got so many pictures of dogs — such good friends, from years and years ago. If the floods have damaged it, I'll never forgive myself."

"It's no use brooding about it, Maude," Val said bracingly. "We'll find out in a day or two, anyway."

Maude nodded, but Neil could see she was still unhappy. He had a collection of pictures of his own — all showing his beloved Sam. He knew how upset he would be if they were lost or damaged.

"The water's going down," he said. "I could get your album for you, if you like."

"Oh, would you? Even if it's already damaged, I'd prefer to get it dried out sooner rather than later."

"Just tell me where to look."

Val hesitated, then pulled out her front door key and gave it to Neil. "I don't want you to take any risks," she said. "But if you can get there, the album is in the top drawer of the cabinet in the living room."

"No problem," said Neil, pocketing the key.

After he let Ludo and Yap out of their pen and put them on their leashes, Neil showed Maude and Val the way through the garden and across the exercise field to the park. Then he joined Emily in the barn.

"What's on your mind?" Emily asked.

Neil explained about Maude's photograph album. "I said I'd get it for her. She looked really upset. It's got pictures of all the dogs she's looked after. Besides, if I go into Compton, I can have another look for Delilah."

"I'll come with you," Emily said. "But you know Mom and Dad won't let us take the boat out by ourselves."

"I don't mean the boat," said Neil. "If the water's going down, it won't be of much help, anyway. We'll walk." He paused, and then added, "We'll tell Mom and Dad that we're taking Jake out. We don't have to tell them where, do we?"

CHAPTER NINE

When Neil and Emily reached the top of the hill where the road led down into Compton, they could already see a big difference. The river had shrunk back to its banks, leaving large stretches of water behind it. Dry ground was visible between them, and although water still covered the main road, it was shallow enough for cars to drive through. The detour signs had been taken away.

Neil and Emily, with Jake walking closely by, skirted the edge of the water along the grassy shoulder of the road.

When they reached Compton, they headed for Maude and Val's house on Windsor Drive, working their way there through streets that were above water level.

Windsor Drive itself was still flooded, though the water didn't come above the tops of their boots. Neil sloshed his way up the path of number 24 and fit the key in the lock. The door stuck, then opened suddenly as Neil pushed against it, so that he was catapulted into the hall.

"Wow!" he said.

The house wasn't underwater anymore, but Neil could see where the floods had been. There was a mark on the walls about three feet up from the floor, and the wallpaper below it was soaked and wrinkled. Water oozed out of the carpet beneath Neil's feet. An umbrella stand and a small table were tipped over on the floor, and the air was filled with a damp smell.

"Hey, hurry up," Emily said as she waited outside with Jake.

Neil investigated the dining room. He had trouble getting the door open. As he pushed it in, he realized that a chair was lying against it. Fortunately, when he got inside, he saw that the top of the cabinet was above the tidemark on the walls, and when he opened the drawer, the album was dry and safe.

He flipped through the pages. The pictures at the back of the album showed Spangle, Ludo, and Yap. On earlier pages, there were others of dogs Neil didn't recognize, some of them photographed with a much younger-looking Maude Lumley. He realized how precious this album must be to her, and how many memories it held. Tucking it under one arm, he went out again and pulled the door shut behind him.

They were ready to go home, but as they were wading back down the path a black taxi drove slowly along the street, leaving a wake behind it like a boat. It stopped a few houses farther down.

"Oh, no!" said Emily. "It's the Jepsons!"

The taxi door opened, and a flurry of wild yapping came out of it. Neil rolled his eyes. "Mrs. Jepson and her little cuddly-wuddlies," he said. "That's all we need!"

The Jepsons' two spoiled little Westies, Sugar and Spice, were the Parkers' least favorite dogs. Neil would have preferred to avoid the Jepsons altogether, but they had to pass the house, and as they came closer to the taxi, Mrs. Jepson got out with Sugar in her arms.

"My beautiful house!" she exclaimed. "My new extension! Ruined!"

Mrs. Jepson was a plump woman with dyed blond hair. She was wearing a bright pink dress and jacket, and she held up her skirts with one hand while she tiptoed up the path in a vain attempt to keep the water from ruining her suede boots.

Mr. Jepson followed her, carrying Spice. He was a tall man with a bony face and he looked even gloomier than usual.

Mrs. Jepson put Sugar down on the step while she rummaged in her bag for her door key. As the taxi pulled away, Sugar launched herself into the water and splashed across the front yard, barking furiously, as if she was trying to chase it. Mr. Jepson tried to head her off and nearly lost his balance.

Suddenly, Sugar's barking turned to frightened whimpers. She was out of her depth, her front paws working frantically to keep herself afloat.

Neil leaped forward.

Mrs. Jepson started to shriek. Mr. Jepson began sloshing his way across the yard, but he was hampered by Spice, who was wriggling in his arms. Sugar was still splashing helplessly, unable to find her feet.

Neil realized that the overweight little Westie was so out of shape that she couldn't keep on struggling for long. Already she was growing weaker.

As Neil got closer, he realized that she must have run into the garden pond. He could just see the top of the cap and the fishing rod of Mrs. Jepson's lawn gnome.

Jake started to bark. He shot ahead, passing Mr. Jepson, and hurled himself at the drowning Westie in the pond.

Sugar let out a yelp as Jake clamped his jaws onto the scruff of her neck. The young Border collie kept his head above water until Neil reached the edge of the pond and hauled them both to safety.

"Good save, Jake!" he said. "Good boy!"

"He's a real hero," said Emily as she caught up. "Again!"

Neil picked up the soggy bundle of white fur and carried her back to Mrs. Jepson, who was still shrieking on the step. Mrs. Jepson folded Sugar into her arms as dirty floodwater soaked into her pink dress.

"Did the nasty dog bite Mummy's diddums, then?" she said.

"Now wait a minute . . ." Emily exclaimed indignantly.

Neil gaped, and then shrugged, grinning. He hadn't really expected Mrs. Jepson to thank him, or Jake. Jake just gave himself a thorough shake, spattering the remaining few spots of Mrs. Jepson's dress that Sugar had missed.

Mr. Jepson came up the front steps and opened the front door. His wife let out another shriek. "Just look at my wallpaper!"

Neil looked. The big pink roses on the walls had turned a muddy brown where the water had been. Mrs. Jepson stared helplessly, and exclaimed, "My furniture! My doggy statuettes!" then vanished into the front room.

"Well, I guess we'll be going," said Neil. "But I think you should shut the door so the dogs don't get out again."

"Don't tell me what to do, young man," Mr. Jepson said, giving Neil an unfriendly stare. "I'll have you know this is the second time I've been flooded out."

"The second?" Neil didn't know what Mr. Jepson was talking about.

"I also had to leave my office in the town hall. After we spent Monday morning moving all the files upstairs, we had to leave by the fire escape. In a boat!"

Mr. Jepson obviously felt very annoyed about his undignified exit. He looked down at Jake snuffling his feet. He shooed the collie away. "*And* there was a dog running around underfoot," he grumbled, almost as an afterthought.

"A dog?" Neil said. He flashed a look at Emily. "What dog?"

"How do I know what dog?" Mr. Jepson said. "It shouldn't have been there. There's a sign on the door that quite clearly says *No Dogs.*"

"Maybe the dog couldn't read," Emily murmured.

Neil was starting to feel more and more excited. He knew he was on to something. "Mr. Jepson," he said, "what did the dog look like?"

For a second, he thought Mr. Jepson wasn't going to answer. Then he pointed to Jake and said abruptly, "Like that."

He retreated into the hall and slammed the door in Neil's face. But Neil didn't care. He didn't need to ask any more questions. He turned to Emily, feeling his face break into an enormous grin of triumph and relief.

"Yes!" he exclaimed. "We've found Delilah!"

CHAPTER TEN

"**J**ake knew all along!" Emily exclaimed. "You knew your mom was in the town hall, didn't you, boy?"

Neil and Emily were heading for the center of Compton. Neil bent down to give Jake a pat.

"We should have listened to you, Jake," he said. "We could have rescued Delilah yesterday."

Jake looked back at him as if to say, "I told you so!"

"But why in the world would she have gone to the town hall?" said Neil.

"I bet she went there because she found a door open," said Emily. "It sounds as if they were all running around in a panic. Nobody would have taken a second look at a dog."

The water in Compton's Market Square was still

much deeper than in Windsor Drive. No one was around, and the town hall looked shut up and deserted.

"How are we going to get in?" Emily asked. "And what if somebody catches us?"

"Then we tell them about Delilah," Neil said determinedly. "I'm not going to let anything stop us now."

They began to cross the market square toward the town hall. Neil felt the floodwater slosh over the tops of his boots and trickle down to his feet. It felt cold as it soaked into his jeans. "The things I do for dogs!"

Jake had to swim in the deepest part of the water, but he reached the town hall without trouble and shook himself vigorously while Neil and Emily squelched up the steps to the main doors.

Neil pushed as hard as he could, but the massive doors stayed shut. "Locked," he muttered.

He took a step back and looked up at the building. He was thinking about breaking a window to get inside. His mom and dad would have a fit if they knew, but finding someone who had keys could take all day, and maybe that was time Delilah didn't have. They didn't know what condition she was in after being abandoned for so many days.

"Mr. Jepson said the staff came down the fire escape," Emily reminded him. "That's probably around the back."

Neil led the way along the side of the building and around the corner into the narrow street behind. The fire escape was an iron staircase bolted to the wall.

"Let's give it a shot," said Neil.

Jake hopped eagerly up the iron steps. As Neil joined him on the ground-floor landing, he saw that the door leading into the building wasn't quite closed. A bulky envelope was wedged in it, as if someone had dropped it on their way out.

"Great!" he said, reaching for the door handle.

"Hang on a minute," Emily said. "What about burglar alarms?"

"What about them?" said Neil. "If they go off, they go off. We're not doing anything wrong."

He pushed, and the door swung open. There was no sound. Cautiously, Neil and Emily made their way inside.

They stood at the end of a long corridor, with doors leading off on either side. The only light came from the doorway where they were standing, and when Neil tried to switch on the lights, nothing happened.

"They must have turned off the electricity," Emily whispered. "Because of the water."

For a second, Neil wondered why she was whispering, but it wasn't hard to guess. The whole place was spooky. He took a deep breath and raised his voice. "Delilah! Hey, Delilah!"

Nothing. Slowly, Neil and Emily began to move down the corridor, checking the rooms on either side.

Jake pattered along beside them, nose to the floor as if he was trying to pick up Delilah's scent.

Most of the rooms were offices, but when Neil opened one door, he let out a long whistle. "Come and look at this, Em!"

Emily was soon peering over his shoulder.

Inside was a large room with a long, polished table down the middle of it. Leather chairs stood all around it, and there were notepads at every place. Neil imagined the mayor and the local councilmen sitting around it, deciding the future of Compton. But he didn't stop for long — Delilah wasn't there, and that was all that mattered.

They checked all of the first floor of the town hall without finding the Border collie, and paused by the stairs.

"Which way now?" Emily asked.

Neil glanced down. Some distance below, he could see debris on the stairs, showing how far the water had risen. If Delilah had been trapped on the ground floor, she might have drowned. Neil didn't want to think about that. "Up," he said.

They checked the second floor, and then the third. There was no sign of Delilah, and no answering bark when they called her name.

"It's no good," Emily said, pushing hair out of her eyes. "She's not here. Maybe she went out again."

"She's got to be here," Neil said stubbornly. Glancing around, he saw Jake scratching at a small door they hadn't checked yet. "What's through there?" Neil asked. "What have you found, boy?"

He gave the door a push. It swung outward, and a cold blast of air came in. The door led out onto the roof.

"She can't be out there," said Emily. "The door was shut."

"Yes, but you can push it open," Neil pointed out. "Maybe it shut behind her and she couldn't get back in."

Neil took a step outside. He stood in a narrow channel between two slate-covered roofs sloping away from him. On the left, a weather vane creaked in the wind. Jake nosed out behind him and let out a sharp bark.

"Keep Jake in there," Neil said. "If he —"

Neil broke off. He thought he had heard a faint whimpering in reply to Jake's bark. "Delilah!" he yelled. "Delilah!"

This time he was sure that he heard a feeble barking. His face lit up and he turned to Emily. "She *is* here!"

"But *where* is she?" Emily was looking relieved and worried at the same time. "I can hear her, but I can't see her. Maybe I should call the fire department."

"Maybe, but I'm going to look," Neil said. "Hang on to Jake. It could be dangerous out here."

Emily crouched in the doorway and put her arms

around Jake. "Be careful," she said, unable to tear herself away from Neil's brave rescue attempt.

Neil began to walk cautiously along the channel between the sloping roofs. He knew Delilah was somewhere on his left, but he didn't know how to reach her, or how she had gotten there in the first place. The slopes looked too steep to climb.

Ahead of him the channel stopped where another part of the roof sloped down to meet it. Neil realized, frustrated, that he had come to a dead end. Maybe he should go back and try to find another way out.

Then he saw that there was debris piled at the foot of where the two slopes met, and one or two holes where slates were missing. A frightened dog might have been able to climb up there.

"And where she can go, I can go," Neil muttered to himself.

He began to scale the roof. His boots slipped on dead leaves and scraps of debris, and he felt another slate give way under him, but he managed to claw his way upward until he could grip the decorated stonework that topped the apex of the roof.

He lifted his head and looked around. All of Compton was spread out below him, looking very small and remote. The sight made Neil feel dizzy, and he quickly shut his eyes. When he opened them again, he made sure he only looked at what was right in front of him.

The roof sloped down again. At the bottom was a

large, flat square, and in the middle of it rose a stone structure that looked a bit like a church spire and held the town clock. At the top was the weather vane.

"Delilah!" shouted Neil.

The bark was repeated, and Neil saw movement at the bottom of the spire. A black nose poked out, followed by Delilah's familiar black-and-white head. She barked again.

"Oh, Delilah!" Neil said. "We've found you at last!"

Delilah crept out from under the clock, took a few unsteady steps toward Neil, and collapsed. She whined unhappily. Neil could see that she was too weak to climb up to him by herself.

Pulling himself up, he brought one leg over the apex of the roof so that he sat straddling it. He was a long way from the edge, but he couldn't help thinking how far it would be to fall. He quickly swung the other leg over so that he could slide down the other side.

He greeted Delilah with a big hug. She was damp and shivering, but she licked his hand feebly in response.

"Come on, girl," he said. "I can't carry you over there. You've *got* to make an effort!"

Pushing Delilah in front of him, Neil managed to scramble up after her. Carefully he guided her over the top and watched with relief as she slid safely down to the channel below.

He heard Emily crying out, "Delilah! Here, girl!"

Closing his eyes tightly, he pulled himself across the apex of the roof and followed Delilah down to safety, with bits of trash and slate scattering under his feet. When he was down, with the open door in front of him, he realized he was shaking, and his mouth went dry at the thought of what he had just done.

Emily kneeled in the doorway with her arms around Delilah. Jake was nuzzling his mom, and although Delilah was very weak, she managed to greet him with a lick.

Emily looked up at Neil as he came back inside and shut the door behind him. "She's safe! She's really safe," she said, then added, "and you're filthy."

Neil looked down at himself. The front of his parka and his jeans were soaked through and stained with dirt and streaks of moss from the roof. He didn't care. "Come on," he said. "We've got to get Delilah home."

"She's too weak to walk that far," Emily said. "We'll have to phone Dad."

Neil knew she was right. He'd imagined sneaking in and sneaking out again so that no one would know what they had done, but now he had to admit that wasn't possible. If they got into trouble, they would just have to face it. But that wasn't important. What mattered was that Delilah was safe.

When Neil and Emily got home, driven by Bob Parker in the Range Rover, they found Mike Turner already at the kennel. Neil carried Delilah carefully through the gate and into the courtyard as the vet was coming out of the dog clinic with Carole.

"I don't think you need worry about the Rough collie," he was saying. "He was just a little shocked and scared by what has been happening. And with the floods going down, you should be able to find his owner soon."

"He ate a little this morning," Carole said. "And he drank some water." Then she saw Neil with Delilah and hurried across the courtyard to him.

"You've really found her!" she said. "Bring her into the kitchen. Jane's waiting."

When Neil and the others crowded into the kitchen, Jane Hammond sprang up from her seat at the table.

"Delilah! Oh, Delilah, you silly girl. Where have you been?"

Her voice was choking, and there were tears in her eyes. Gently, she took Delilah from Neil's arms and laid her down on some old blankets spread on the floor in front of the stove. She stroked Delilah's head while Mike Turner examined her carefully. Jake pushed in beside Jane to sniff his mom and nuzzle her comfortingly.

Everyone else gathered around to watch. Delilah lay quietly, but her eyes were bright and she was starting to take an interest in what was around her.

At last, Mike Turner straightened up. Neil felt suddenly relieved as he saw that the vet was smiling.

"She's fine," the vet said. "Nothing wrong with her at all that a good rest in a warm basket won't cure. And watch her diet for the next couple of days. . . . Don't give her too much to eat at once. If you're at all worried, give me a call."

"Thank you," said Jane. She couldn't take her eyes off Delilah, who was looking up at her with a contented, trusting expression, as if she knew everything would be all right now that she was back with her beloved owner. "But, Neil, where was she? How did you manage to find her?"

Neil had been waiting for this moment. He wanted to burst out laughing at Jane's amazed expression as he said, "On the town hall roof, under the clock."

"It was Jake who found her," Emily added. "He knew all along!"

"Well, thank you, Jake," said Jane, giving the young dog a pat.

"I'm going to make him a medal," said Sarah. "He's the smartest dog in the world!"

On Saturday, a stiff breeze was blowing, sending the clouds scudding across the sky. There were some blue patches, and sometimes the sun shone out, but rain still fell in short, sharp showers.

Neil stood outside the barn at King Street Kennels and watched Jake and Noah chasing each other across the grass. He was looking after the little brown dog while Greg and Joanne Forrester served the party food inside.

"This is great," said Emily.

Through the open doors of the barn, Neil could see Mike Turner, Alex Harvey with his dogs, Finn and Sandy, Gavin Thorpe with Jet, and lots of other Compton friends who had come to celebrate Bob and Carole's fifteenth wedding anniversary — and the tenth anniversary of King Street Kennels.

Jane and Richard Hammond were there, too, with Delilah, who already looked much more like her old self.

"Look at your mom, Jake," Neil said as the young Border collie scampered past with Noah snapping playfully at his tail. "Isn't she terrific?"

As Neil watched, Maude Lumley and Val Jennings came out through the doors with glasses in their hands and Maude's three dogs walking obediently at heel. Each dog was beautifully groomed; even Spangle hadn't managed to get herself muddy yet.

"We went home yesterday," Val told Neil and Emily. "And you wouldn't believe the mess! But it's good to be back."

"And to have the dogs with us again," Maude said, with a fond smile at her three friends. "Neil, I can't tell you how grateful I am to you for bringing me my album."

"It was Em, too," Neil said, feeling himself beginning to turn red. In all the excitement of finding Delilah, he had completely forgotten about the photograph album. For all he knew, it could have been abandoned in the town hall. But Emily had kept it safe, and Bob had delivered it to Maude at her hotel.

"Then thank you both," said Maude. "And I hope you have a lovely day."

"We will!" said Emily.

As Maude and Val strolled away over the grass, Neil saw Max making his way through the crowds of guests toward the barn doors. He had a plate of food in his hand.

The young actor had arrived in Compton only that morning by train, with Prince, his cocker spaniel, and Princess, his adorable golden pup.

"Aren't you going to get something to eat?" Max asked. "The food's fantastic!"

"Lead me to it!" said Neil.

He was just heading inside when he heard a banging noise and saw his mom's brother, Jack Tansley, appear over the heads of the crowd. He was standing on a chair near the doors, waiting for everybody to be quiet.

"I've been asked to say a few words," he began. "I'm absolutely delighted to be here today to celebrate Carole and Bob's anniversary. Not just to remember the day they got married, but also the day they opened King Street Kennels.

"I think that everybody here knows how much Carole and Bob have done for dogs in Compton, and I know you'll agree with me when I say that Compton would be worse off without them and their family.

"So I'd like to ask you to raise your glasses and drink a toast to Carole and Bob, and wish them many more happy and — dare I say it? — dog-filled years at King Street Kennels. To Carole and Bob!"

The guests drank the toast and clapped enthusiastically. There was a chorus of barking from the dogs, and Mr. Hamley's crazy Dalmatian, Dotty, leaped up at him and nearly knocked him off his chair.

Neil was laughing. "This is a riot!" he said.

As he made his way into the barn, there was a sudden spatter of raindrops.

"Look!" said Emily.

Neil followed her pointing finger. Past the house, in the direction of Compton, the sky was filled with a bright rainbow. As he gazed at it, Neil was sure that the floods, and all the trouble they had caused, were really, truly over.